SHADOWS WAR

THE CRYSTAL OF UNITY
SHADOWS WAR

BOOK ONE

KATIE L. POTH

TATE PUBLISHING
AND **ENTERPRISES**, LLC

Shadows War
Copyright © 2014 by Katie L. Poth. All rights reserved.

No part of this publication may be reproduced, stored in a retrieval system or transmitted in any way by any means, electronic, mechanical, photocopy, recording or otherwise without the prior permission of the author except as provided by USA copyright law.

The opinions expressed by the author are not necessarily those of Tate Publishing, LLC.

Published by Tate Publishing & Enterprises, LLC
127 E. Trade Center Terrace | Mustang, Oklahoma 73064 USA
1.888.361.9473 | www.tatepublishing.com

Tate Publishing is committed to excellence in the publishing industry. The company reflects the philosophy established by the founders, based on Psalm 68:11,
"The Lord gave the word and great was the company of those who published it."

Book design copyright © 2014 by Tate Publishing, LLC. All rights reserved.
Cover design by Joel Uber
Interior design by Jomar Ouano

Published in the United States of America

ISBN: 978-1-62746-925-8
1. Fiction / Fantasy / General
2. Fiction / Action & Adventure
13.12.12

Dedication

To my five amazing children, Micale (my inspiration for this series), Aden Kai, Hadassah, Evan Oliver and Abigail. They are all my perfect gifts from God and true blessings every day!

Contents

Prologue 9

The Mystery Visitor 15
Road Trip 25
Treasure To Be Found 33
The Evening Heat 43
Dragon World 57
The Explanation 65
Destiny Unfolds 75
Prophecy Lies Ahead 85
The First Encounter 93
Triumphant Return 101
Smells Like Danger 107
Home Again 115

Prologue

Ryan sat on the edge of his bed as his grandpa twirled around in a bed sheet cape and plunged his cardboard sword toward imaginary danger. The struggle was intense; who would achieve victory? It was a battle of good and evil, a story as old as time itself. The fate of Dragon World was in the balance. The dark one could not be allowed to get her claws on the queen. The future of the land was within the queen; a gallant prince was prophesied to be born unto her; a prince who would once and for all end the reign of Darkness.

"I came against the ferocious beast and cried out for Ashmond," said Grandpa with excitement as the story intensified. "Her wings raised high into the sky and I could hear the sound of fire brewing within her. I was as good as gone. I held out my sword and began to plunge it toward the beast. I had a chance for but one last mighty blow. I prepared to face certain death when I suddenly felt myself begin to rise up from the ground. I heard the familiar cry of my comrade as I saw the glow of fire beneath us. He had saved me in battle once again. Together we would fight, together we shall win."

Ryan clasped his hands together in excitement, bouncing in the edge of the bed.

"Ashmond circled around and yelled for me to make ready," Grandpa continued. "I held out my sword, now confident and true. Darkness, knowing her time was short, made one last attempt to capture the queen and ensure her victory over Dragon World. She let out a ball of fire and disappeared into the smoke. 'She is headed for the castle!' I exclaimed to Ashmond. 'We must hurry and save the queen!' Ashmond flew with speed, intent to save his beloved queen. For she was not only his queen, but his wife, and it was his son she carried."

"Upon the castle gates we saw Darkness. We knew she must be stopped, and there was only one way. I made my way toward Ashmond's tail. '"Are you sure about this?"' Ashmond questioned. '"It's our only hope,"' I answered with confidence. Ashmond nodded. I knew it was a dangerous move, but it was also one that Darkness would never suspect."

Ryan scooted even closer to the edge if the bed. He could hardly contain himself. This was one of Grandpa's most exciting stories yet!

"What were you planning on doing?" yelled Ryan, completely overwhelmed with excitement.

Grandpa, unaffected by his outburst, continued with the story. "We neared the castle just as Darkness was overcoming the front guards. Ashmond positioned himself around the thick trees that lined the castle walls. I braced myself and held my sword firmly out over my head. I locked my arms and gave Ashmond a wink to signal that I was ready. With a mighty swing of his tail, I was off!"

"I turned and twisted my body to fly directly toward my target. I could hardly breathe as the air whipped past me. I was flying with such speed that sound seem to disappear. Soon enough, sound did return. It returned with the shrill cries of my mortally wounded enemy. Darkness never saw me coming toward her.

My sword penetrated deep within her heart. I fell to the ground; my body now weak."

"As I lay on the cold hard ground my eyes fluttered open. I saw Darkness clinch the wound that I had bestowed upon her. She flared her large thick nostrils at me and staggered closer. I lay helpless, unable to move. I could feel her warm breath on my skin."

Ryan slipped off the edge of the bed and fell to the floor in his knees. His face showed the concern that raced through him.

"I knew this was it. I was about to be toast!" Grandpa said playfully, building Ryan's anticipation

"What happened?" Ryan shouted in a panic.

"Well," replied Grandpa, "nothing."

Ryan's face squished up with befuddlement.

Grandpa continued, "I opened my eyes to see Darkness fly away, then I drifted off into unconsciousness. She must have known that she was fatally wounded. I was peaceful with the thought that we had won. Dragon World was safe."

"Hooray!" Ryan shouted as he jumped up and down. "Dragon World is safe!"

Suddenly, the bedroom door flew opened. "What is going on in here?" asked Ryan's mom as she stared them down with her big, brown eyes. "I thought you were just going to tell him good night before you and Grandma headed home?"

"I am," replied Grandpa as he quickly removed his bed sheet cape, placed it over Ryan, and flung him back into his bed. "I'm just tucking him in now."

"Okay," said Mom, finding it hard not to smile a little at Grandpa's childlike attitude. "Just remember, it's a school night." She closed the door behind her and went back down the stairs.

"Well, I guess I better let you get to sleep," said Grandpa as he pulled up the blanket and tucked it in around Ryan.

"Oh, but I can't sleep now," said Ryan, "I want to hear more about Dragon World!"

"Ryan," replied his grandpa softly, "one day you will go to Dragon World with me. It is your destiny to serve alongside the prince, just as I have served his father and just as my grandfather served his father. Our family has served the Kings of Dragon World for generations. It is our legacy."

Grandpa kissed Ryan on the head and walked toward the door. "You will be a great warrior one day, I can see it in your valiant green eyes." He turned off the light and closed the door. Ryan fell fast asleep with visions of dragons and swords, unaware of what was to come.

The Mystery Visitor

Ryan tapped his pencil on the desk as he stared at the old clock that hung on the dingy classroom wall. He gazed at the black hands of the clock, waiting for the long hand to pass the number 6 six, triggering the very welcomed chime of the school bell. Oh, how he longed to hear the school bell ring through the halls for the last time this year!

The anticipation of summer vacation could be felt throughout the halls. Even the teacher had his keys in hand and vaguely resembled a racehorse chomping at the bit, waiting for the sound of the gun. Ryan looked around the classroom at everyone. They were all anxious to hear the bell ring, for when it did, not only did it mean long lazy summer days, but that they would officially be middle schoolers!

Ryan began to become very anxious at the thought of starting middle school. He knew he needed a distraction from that thought, so he reached over to his tattered blue jean backpack that sat upon the worn floor and pulled out a large red notebook. He drew to help pass the time.

He always carried a notebook with him to draw and journal in, and dragons were his favorite subject matter. He based them on the whimsical stories that his grandpa had told him. Whenever he had visited with his grandparents, Grandpa told him elaborate tales of the magical Dragon World where dragons ruled, and an epic battle was raging. He would tell of how he saved the Royal dragon family many times from an evil dragon force known only by the name of Darkness.

Darkness hated the Royal Dragon Family. She despised their love for each other and their subjects, but most of all she hated their love for the human race. Darkness did not believe that dragons and humans should be considered equal. She believed that dragons were more powerful than feeble little humans; and, therefore, humans should bow down and worship dragons, especially her.

Ryan loved those stories and the memories of the time spent with his grandpa. Grandpa was quite the performer too. He could turn just about anything into a prop. Once he even used Ryan's retainer as ferocious dragon teeth. It was the first and only time that a retainer had ever been cool.

Ryan looked down at a blank piece of notebook paper and began to draw a picture of Ashmond, king of the dragons and Grandpa's dragon counterpart. Grandpa spoke of him in great detail, with such power and respect that Ryan would almost forget that he was just a character in a story.

As Ryan began to draw Ashmond's eyes, he leaned in close to the paper and moved his pencil carefully. He always made sure that they were the eyes of a dragon that had fought great wars, but still loved as though he had never seen evil, like the love he saw in Grandpa's eyes.

Ryan sketched the final details and slowly pulled the pencil away. As he studied the drawing, he felt drawn into the eyes. For a moment, he could have sworn that he saw them move, as if the picture was coming to life! He leaned in closer for a better look. He felt his heart begin to race and the room became very warm. Suddenly, he felt a wet sting on the back of his head that quickly pulled him back to the small warm classroom. He sat straight up in his chair and ran his fingers through his dark-brown hair and soon came across a spitball behind his left ear. He turned and saw Tovi and Eli snickering and pointing.

"Were you just kissing that dragon?" taunted Eli.

"Ryan, the dragon bride!" added Tovi, not to be outdone by Eli.

I am certainly not going to miss them this summer, he thought as he turned and slid down deep into his chair, as most of the class began to laugh.

Ryan looked over toward Ellie as she turned another page in her book. She seemed to be the only person in class that was not gearing up to dart for the door the minute the bell rang, or laughing at him. Ryan knew she would not be laughing at him. Ellie is his best friend, even though they were very different. Ellie like to say that they were perfect friends because they complemented each other's personalities. She was popular, smart, beautiful, loved sports, and –

though Ryan was quiet, clumsy, and rather awkward–she always treated him like he was something special.

Ryan started to drift off as he focused on her long blonde hair, which was tied up with a pink ribbon. She always wore a ribbon in her hair, ever since kindergarten. Her mother passed away when Ellie was just five years old. She was in a car accident while Ellie was at school. It was the first day of Kindergarten and her mom had tied a blue ribbon in her hair to match her pretty blue dress. Her mom was so proud of her that day and it was the last time Ellie saw her. Ever since then, she always put a ribbon in her hair. Ellie said it was a way to stay close to her mom.

Ryan had lived next door to Ellie his whole life. They had always been best friends, but lately Ryan had begun to look at her a little differently. He had started to notice just how blue her eyes are. He began to think about those blue eyes when suddenly—Ring! Ring! Ring! The bell cried out, and everyone jumped to their feet. It caught Ryan by surprise and he fell from his chair giving everyone one last good laugh as they headed for the door.

Yep, thought Ryan, *that was the perfect way to start my summer.* He grabbed his backpack, shoved his notebook inside, and headed for the door.

As Ryan was walking home, daydreaming of how he would be spending his summer vacation, Tovi and Eli whipped past him on their skateboards, grabbing his backpack from his shoulder and knocking him to the cold concrete sidewalk.

Ryan let out a heavy sigh as he stood up and dusted off his jeans, "Very funny, guys. You got me. May I have my backpack now, please?"

"Come and get it," taunted Tovi as he sped away around the corner.

Ryan sighed again and set out to run after him, but as he came to the corner he heard a loud thump. When he rounded the corner he was surprised to see Ellie standing there holding his tattered blue jean backpack!

"You're welcome," she said with a smirk. Ryan looked past her in disbelief as he reached for his backpack.

He saw Tovi on the ground rolling in pain while Eli was standing over him laughing and shouting, "You just got taken down by a girl!"

Ryan's jaw dropped. "What? How did you…?" he stuttered as he stood stunned.

"Come on Ryan," Ellie replied as she wrapped her arm in his and led him away. "Walk me home."

As Ellie and Ryan approached their houses, they noticed a strange car in Ryan's driveway. "Whose car is that?" Ellie asked.

"I'm not sure," replied Ryan as he peered toward the driveway with curiosity.

"You better get home then," said Ellie as she headed up the path to her front door. "Call me later."

"I will," replied Ryan halfheartedly, as he crept toward the strange black car to inspect it a little closer.

Hmm, he thought as he peered inside looking for clues as to who this mystery visitor might be. He half hoped to see some signs of a straitjacket or boarding school brochure, revealing that his parents may have finally come to their senses about allowing his sister to remain in the house. All he saw was an oversized pink sun hat on the front seat along with a large pink and white polka dot purse. A beam of light caught his eye, causing him to raise his hand to block its gleam. He squinted a bit. *What was that?* He leaned in for a better look. There was a medallion hanging from the rear view mirror, but not just any medallion,

"Ashmond," Ryan whispered to himself.

Ryan filled with excitement as all the pieces came together. He dashed inside as fast as he could.

"Grandma!" he yelled as he rushed through the living room and into the kitchen. "Grandma!" he yelled once again as he threw his arms around her plump waist.

He loved hugging her. She was soft and warm and always smelled like a cupcake. She kind of resembled one too; she was short and round and had a way of making everyone smile when she was in the room.

"My little Ryan!" she exclaimed as she squeezed him tightly. "Oh, you aren't so little any more, are you?" she stated as she stepped back to get a better look at him. "I am much too young to have a grown man for a grandson, and so handsome, just like your grandfather!" she exclaimed.

Ryan puffed out his chest. "I've grown a whole foot taller since you last saw me," Ryan announced proudly.

"The only thing you've grown is more annoying," teased Isabel, Ryan's older sister, as she walked into the room, running her thin freckled fingers through her frizzy red hair. Grandpa always joked that her temper was as fiery as her hair. "Now go and get packed, and don't bring any of your nerdy dragon dolls with you," she continued.

"Packed?" asked Ryan, ignoring her comment about his highly collectible (and totally awesome) dragon figures. "Where are we going?"

"With me, dear," replied his grandmother with excitement. "Isn't it great? You and Isabel are going to stay with me for the whole summer!"

"Why?" asked Ryan as he filled with a little bit of sorrow over the thought of being away from Ellie for the whole summer. "I mean, um, why am I just finding out about this now?"

"Grandma won a trip to Hawaii," replied his mom with a huge smile. "And she gave the trip to your father and me! Isn't that great? Hawaii, can you believe it?"

Ryan felt a little sick to his stomach as his mom began to do the hula.

"I've already been to Hawaii two times," explained Grandma. "So I traded them the trip for a summer with my grandchildren."

"The *whole* summer?" asked Ryan.

"Why yes, dear," replied Grandma a bit puzzled. "I thought you would be excited. After all, it's been such a long time since I've had you for a visit. We have a lot of time to make up for." She leaned in close to Ryan, "And I have a very special surprise for you."

"I am excited. It's just that… well…I…," he stuttered.

"He's just doesn't want to be away from his precious Ellie," Isabel teased.

Ryan felt his face grow red. "No, that's not it!" he shouted.

"Oh," replied Grandma with a smirk on her face. "Well I think she is a fine choice. I always thought that she was special. As you know, your grandpa and I grew up together as best friends too."

"Choice, what choice?" choked Ryan. "No choice! We are just friends! End of story!"

Ryan, now mortified, hung his head and darted to his room, while his sister made smooching noises and began to sing about Ryan and Ellie in a tree K-I-S-S-I-N-G. He was in his room before the baby carriage came.

Road Trip

Early the t loading the luggage in his grandmother's car when he heard a very welcomed voice.

"Hi Ryan," said Ellie as she walked up to him. Her long blonde hair was in a red bow today. It matched her red shoes. Ryan thought red was beautiful on her. Of course, he thought just about every color looked beautiful on her.

"Hey," he replied, his voice cracking a little bit.

"Are you going somewhere?" she asked. "You never called me last night. Who does the car belong to?"

"My grandma came in for a surprise visit," he answered.

"Grandma Drakon?" replied Ellie in a surprised tone.

"Yah," replied Ryan, "it was quite a surprise. She seems to be full of them," he continued in a mumble.

"That certainly is a surprise!" she said, "You haven't seen her since your grandpa went missing. How is she?"

Ryan thought for a moment about his grandpa. He missed him a lot. He had suddenly gone missing nearly a year ago. No one in the family ever spoke about it. His parents would not tell him anything, but he was able to piece together some information by sitting at the top of the stairs, listening to his parents talk in the kitchen. They thought he was asleep in bed, and he knew it was wrong to listen in on others people's conversations, but he needed answers.

All he knew for sure was that Grandpa had gotten up early to go for a walk around the property to check the fences, which he did often, and he never came home. The police came to the house once to ask his parents questions, but he was quickly ushered to his room before he could find out anything of value.

Ryan had trouble believing that Grandpa was gone. He could still remember how he had a smile that would always make everyone laugh; mom called it the grandpa grin. He also had this amazing squeeze of a hug. It was like a bear had gotten a hold of you. Ryan loved those hugs. Grandpa was always making everyone laugh too. He would do funny things, especially out in public. Mom and Grandma would act embarrassed, but they would eventually burst out laughing too.

After Grandpa disappeared, Grandma asked to be alone for a while. It was odd because Ryan and Isabel normally spent a lot of time over there, especially over the summer.

"Ryan?" Ellie said softly as she touched his shoulder. "Did you hear me?

"Oh, yah, sorry," replied Ryan. "She seems to be doing well."

"Are you okay?" she then asked with concern.

"Me? Of course," he replied with pride as he pulled himself together. "I'm just a little tired. I spent most of last night listening to Isabel talk Grandma's ear off about her stupid boyfriend, Trent."

Ellie, realizing that his sad demeanor probably had more to do with missing his grandpa than being tired, began to help Ryan load luggage into the car. "This is a lot of luggage," she remarked as she struggled to get one of Isabel's many suitcases into the trunk.

"Yes, well…um…," Ryan stammered. He was not sure how to tell Ellie that he was going to be away for the whole summer. They had planned to spend their summer together. Ellie's dad worked a lot, and it was very lonely at her house. She liked being over at Ryan's house, even with Isabel there. In fact, she once told Ryan that she wished she had a big sister. Ryan could not understand why she would make such a crazy wish.

"What's wrong?" Ellie asked as she placed her hands on her hips. "You always stutter like that when you don't want to tell me something."

"It's not really bad news. I know we planned on spending the summer together, but Grandma is taking me and Isabel to her house for the summer," Ryan said while rubbing the back of his next anxiously and staring at the pavement. "Really?" replied Ellie with a surprising amount of excitement, "That sounds like so much fun! I love your grandma's house!"

Ellie had gone with Ryan and his family to his grandparents' house many times. She loved to go with Ryan to visit their huge old house and explore all of the antiques. They had stuff from all over the world. They were always off visiting some exotic location. Ellie and Ryan also spent a lot of time out in the barn when they would visit. It had an attic that was just full of all kinds of stuff. Ellie and Ryan would pretend that it was the magical Dragon World that Grandpa would always talk about. Ellie loved to listen to his stories almost as much as Grandpa loved telling them.

"Oh, I wish I could go with you!" she said as she held her hands together and closed her eyes as if she were making a big wish.

Ryan turned to put another suitcase into the car and closed his eyes and secretly made the same wish.

"It's time to hit the road," Grandma shouted as she exited the house.

"Oh Ellie," she exclaimed as she opened her arms to her. "You have grown into such a beautiful young lady! I wouldn't have known it was you had it not been for your beautiful red ribbon."

"Thank you," Ellie exclaimed as she ran toward Grandma's opened arms. "I am so happy to see you again, Grandma Drakon."

"And I you, dear," said Grandma as she hugged her tight.

Ellie stepped back and looked as though she had a tear in her eye. "Well, you all have fun," she said as she ran back toward her house. "I'll see you at the end of summer."

"Bye, Ellie," Ryan yelled as the back door closed behind her. Ryan was a little upset at the way Ellie had just ran off like that. What kind of goodbye was that if they were not going to see each other for nearly three months?

"Come and give me a hug goodbye," ordered Mom, "Dad and I have to leave for the airport soon and Grandma is ready to hit the road."

Ryan gave his mom a hug. "Awe, Mom!" complained Ryan as his mom snuck in a kiss to his forehead. He pretended to wipe it off as he walked over to say goodbye to his dad.

"You take good care of your sister and Grandmother this summer," ordered his dad as he jokingly shook his finger at Ryan.

"Yes sir," replied Ryan while he motioned to salute him as if he were a general in the army. His father laughed and gave him a hug. "Dad," Ryan whined. "Dudes don't hug, they high-five." His dad laughed again and slapped him five.

Ryan looked over at Ellie's house one last time as he climbed into the car. He had hoped she might come back out and say goodbye again, but no such luck. Ryan turned away from the window and slouched down in his seat. He was not looking forward to the two-hour drive to Grandma's house, especially if that two hours included listening to Isabel go on and on about her stupid boyfriend. Trent is so awesome. Trent it so smart. Trent is so blah, blah, blah! Ryan cringed at the thought of the conversation!

Ryan did not like Trent, for many reasons, not the least of which was the fact that Trent is none other than Tovi's older brother. Tovi and Ryan had been enemies ever since kindergarten. Tovi would always break Ryan's crayons and dump his glue all over his desk. The worst was in the first grade, when Tovi dumped milk down the front of Ryan and told the class that Ryan had wet his pants, after that he could not walk the halls without someone yelling, "Look out, here comes Bladder Blaster," whenever he would walk down the halls.

Ryan hated it, but he knew all of that would change next year, when he enters Middle School. It will be a fresh start at a new school. He had also heard from Isabel that Trent and Tovi's dad might be getting transferred and they might be moving to Alaska! Ryan loved picturing Tovi suffering cold in Alaska with nothing to eat but fish. He knew Tovi hated fish. Fish stick day was the only day of the week that Tovi did not steal Ryan's lunch.

Isabel was not at all happy about the idea of Trent possibly moving. She was always crying about it. *Oh, boo hoo,* thought Ryan. Even though he and Isabel did not get along, he still thought even she deserved better than stupid Trent!

As they began to drive away, Isabel of course started to tell Grandma all about Trent. *Ugh*, thought Ryan, *Good thing I have my video games*. He plugged in his earphones and drifted off into game world.

Treasure To Be Found

A little was about to utterly defeat level four and move on to the bonus level –a task he had been looking forward to ever since Tovi had bragged about how he beat it after only six tries–, he suddenly felt a sharp jab on the top of his head.

"Ouch!" he shouted. He looked up to see his sister's angry freckled face glaring at him. Of course, he was use to this, lately she always seemed to look that way.

"What was that for?" he shouted as he removed his headphones from his ears

"Turn off your game," she replied with a snotty tone.

"Why?" he asked in a grouchy tone.

"I would prefer that we not use any electronics during this visit," responded Grandma. "There is so much of the world passing you by when you have your nose glued to a video game." Isabel stuck her tongue out at Ryan and turned back around. "Or your thumbs tapping away at your cell phone," Grandma continued.

"What!" asked Isabel suddenly aware that this new rule affected her as well. "No texting? I didn't sign up for that!"

"In that case," Ryan replied with a smirk." I think it will be easy to give up my video games, watching Isabel suffer through text withdrawals will be all the entertainment I need."

Ryan packed up his videogames and passed them up to Grandma. Isabel reluctantly handed over her cell phone, but not without sending a few quick texts to Trent first.

Ryan sat back in his seat and turned his focus out the window as Isabel was busy listing to Grandma all the reasons why she should be allowed to text, especially to Trent. Ryan was watching all the trees go by and began to feel calm and relaxed. *This is nice,* he thought, *as long as I can tune out Isabel.* Ryan rolled down his window, the noise from the passing air helped to drown her out. *Ah, that's better*, he thought.

He liked the feel of the warm breeze. He stuck his hand out the window and began to watch it glide up and down on the wind currents as though flying. Suddenly something caught his eye and he was stunned by what he saw, or at least what he thought he saw. It appeared to be a small black dragon flying alongside his hand. He jumped back in his seat and froze for a moment.

I didn't just see that, did I? he wondered as he leaned forward and stared out the window.

"We're here!" Grandma sang out, snapping Ryan out of his daze.

Ryan blinked his eyes then looked out the window again, but all he saw were the tall old trees that lined the long driveway to the Draken Plantation. *How did two hours pass by so fast?* he wondered. He shook his head once more, *listening to Isabel must be making me go crazy.*

Ryan shook it off and got out of the car and away from Isabel.

As he entered the big old house, it seemed different without Grandpa there. He glanced at the coat rack by the door and saw Grandpa's favorite baseball cap still hanging there as if it were just waiting to top his salt and pepper head of hair. Ryan closed his eyes and took a deep breath; he could still smell Grandpa's cologne. It was almost as if he were just around the corner in the study.

Ryan looked to the study and heard a noise. *Someone is in there*, he thought to himself. He slowly stepped toward the open study door. He was about to peer inside when he was unexpectedly knocked down to the floor by a mighty blow, followed by some very wet kisses.

Ryan was thrilled when he realized that it was none other than Grandpa's loyal doberman pinscher, Tiger. He looked scary, but he was just an oversized lap dog.

"Tiger!" shouted Ryan between wet kisses, "How are you boy? I sure have missed you!" Ryan and Tiger began to wrestle on the floor when Isabel stormed in.

"Ugh," sighed an extremely annoyed Isabel. "Get up and bring in the luggage," she demanded as she stomped up the stairs to her room.

"I guess Grandma didn't give in to her texting requests," laughed Ryan as he scratched Tiger behind his soft black and tan ear.

After Ryan finished bringing in the luggage and putting away his clothes he ventured downstairs.

He wandered through the large house for a while looking at the photos that hung on the wall. They were mostly of his grandparents travels all over the world. He loved to look at the pictures when he would visit. His grandpa would tell him all kinds of crazy stories about their travels, stories about fighting off evil dragon lord warriors and saving our world from destruction. Grandpa said that the dangers of Dragon World often carried over into our own world, but the coming prince would change all that.

As Ryan came to the end of the hall he saw a picture that caught his eye. He had not seen this one before. It was of his grandpa, but he was very young, about Ryan's age. He was standing in the backyard of the house, close to the barn. Ryan recognized it because that was the same place that Ryan loved to play when he would visit. There is a tree there with a hole in it that Ryan could crawl into. His grandfather had shown it to him the first summer he came to stay without his parents. He was homesick, but after grandpa showed him that fort he had so much fun that the summer seemed to pass by in a day.

Ryan noticed that his grandpa was holding something in the picture, but he could not quite make out what it was. As he studied the object closer he remembered that his grandpa kept a magnifying glass on his desk in the study.

He ran to the study and found the magnifying glass still lying upon the desk. He picked it up and looked at it. He always thought it had a rather odd handle. It looked almost like a large fish scale. Once, while he was walking into the study to see his grandpa, Ryan could have sworn that he even saw it glowing while his grandpa was holding it.

Ryan, with the magnifying glass in hand, turned and ran back down the hall. To his surprise, he found his grandma standing there.

"Where are you off to in such a hurry?" she asked as she placed her hands on his shoulders to slow him to a stop. "I wanted to talk to you about something impor…."

Ryan had a one-tract mind and cut his grandma off. "Do you know anything about this picture of grandpa?" he asked in a hurried voice as he pointed to the picture on the wall.

"Oh, yes, I love this picture," she replied as she took it from the wall and began to wipe dust from the glass with her apron. "I believe he was about your age in this picture," she continued. "And just as excitable as you," she giggled. "It was taken in the backyard. You know, Grandpa grew up in this house, as did his grandfather.

It has been passed down to the eldest grandson for generations, and one day it will be yours."

Ryan loved the idea that he would one day live in this house. His grandpa had told him this many times, especially when he was helping him fix something around the house. "One day this will be yours to fix, so pay attention," he would say.

"It will be time for dinner soon," Grandma said softly as she gently hung the picture back on the wall. "Why don't you go out and play for bit? We will talk later."

Ryan watched his grandmother's face as it seemed to turn pale, he could tell that she missed grandpa very much. He decided he would not ask any more questions about Grandpa right now. He placed the magnifying glass into his pocket, gave her a hug, and then headed outside.

Ryan walked through the tall grass while whipping a stick through the air, as if fighting off imaginary villains. He began to feel the heat of the sun beating down on him, so he looked around the yard for some relief. He then spotted the big tree by the barn. *That will provide some much needed shade for a tired soldier,* he thought.

Ryan ran to the tree and fell to his knees. He crawled around to the far side and looked for the entrance to his secret fort. He gently ran his fingers over the bark; he soon found where Grandpa had carved the words 'The Dragon's Den'. That was what they called their little fort. He felt around a little more until his finger came across where grandpa had helped him carve his name one summer. Ryan still carried the pocketknife that Grandpa had given him to carve it with.

Just below the carving was the opening to the fort. He quickly pulled away some of the dirt and leaves that had piled in front of the opening, then crawled inside.

Once inside it was dark and it took his eyes a moment to adjust after being out in the bright sun. Looking around he thought that it was a bit smaller than he had remembered. Of course, he was a bit taller now. He was also a little disappointed because it just did not seem as magical as it had in the past.

Ryan began to run his hand across the cool ground when he felt something across his fingers. It felt like a warm piece of glass. He felt for it again. As his fingers passed over the object again, it began to glow red.

What is that?, he thought to himself in awe.

He pulled his hand back, not sure what it was, but as soon as he did the light went out. *Weird*, he thought. He felt for it again. This time he saw that it was caught under a root of the tree. He pulled the pocketknife from his pocket and used the handle to gently pry the object from the ground. As he touched it, it once again began to glow red.

Ryan crawled out into the sun to get a better look at what he had found. He began to examine it closely when a loud boom of thunder made him jump!. A flash of lightning then danced across the ever darkening sky. The sun was quickly engulfed as dark storm clouds rolled in.

Ryan heard his grandma call, "Come in before you get caught in the rain. I have a surprise for you!"

Ryan quickly put the *intriguing* red object into his pocket and ran toward the house.

The Evening Heat

Ryan ran into the house, but he did not quite escape the rain. As he stood in the doorway, shaking raindrops from his shirt and hair, he heard a surprising sound. "You didn't have to shower for me."

"Ellie!" Ryan gasped with amazement. "What are you doing here?"

"My dad had a business trip," she replied with excitement. "He asked your mom to watch me while he was gone, but since she was on her way to Hawaii, she called your grandma and here I am!"

Ryan was so happy, *Wishes do come true,* he thought. He quickly tried to hide his delight, so as to not give Grandma any ideas. He could already see her planning the wedding as she watched them.

"That's not fair," whined Isabel. "Ryan can have a friend stay, but I can't even send a text to Trent?"

Grandma ignored Isabel's tantrum. "You two go upstairs and get ready for dinner," she said as she headed in to the dining room to set the table.

Isabel followed her, stomping her feet like a child while begging for her cell phone back.

Ellie and Ryan looked at each other and laughed. "Looks like you were in need of reinforcements," giggled Ellie. "It's a good thing I came." The two friends headed up the stairs to clean up for dinner.

After dinner, as Isabel and Grandma were cleaning the dishes, Ryan and Ellie were sent upstairs to get ready for bed. Ellie had the room across the hall from him. They called it the blue room, for obvious reasons.

"Goodnight, Ryan," yawned Ellie, as she stood in the doorway to her room. "I'll see you bright and early," she continued sleepily. "We have dragons to tend to."

Ryan smiled at the memory of the games they would play in the attic of the barn. "Good night Ellie," he replied as he slowly closed the door to his room.

In his room, Ryan went to hop into bed when the glossy, red object he had found in the old fort fell from his pocket. He knelt down and picked it up off the old wood floor. It was still rather dirty, so he went to the bathroom and began to run water over it from the sink. As the dirt washed away he noticed that it was a crystal of some sort. It kind of reminded him of the garnet stones in grandma and grandpas wedding rings. He wiped it down with a cloth and saw that it looked to be in the shape of a dragon.

Bam! Bam! Bam!

"Get out of the bathroom," demanded his sister urgently. "I need it!"

A startled Ryan nearly dropped the figure. "Alright, alright!" he replied as he put the crystal back into his pocket and opened the door. "All yours, your royal pain in the butt," he continued, as he bowed to her while holding the door.

"Whatever," she replied. "Grandma wants you to take out the garbage from the kitchen." She entered the bathroom, still mumbling something under her breath about wanting to text Trent.

"Perhaps her text withdrawals aren't going to be so entertaining," Ryan shrugged as he hurried down stairs.

Ryan grabbed the garbage bags and headed out the door toward the barn, where the cans were kept until Grandma went to the dump. He stuffed them in and quickly replaced the lids. The smell was quite strong! *Ugh, it smells like Isabel's cooking*, he thought to himself as he chuckled at the memory of Isabel trying to make sushi one night. She thought she could blend Mexican and sushi. It was a defiantly *not* a good combination!

As he headed back toward the house he heard a noise coming from the barn. He turned and looked, but saw nothing. *Must be raccoons looking for a snack*, he thought. He then looked up at the stars gleaming over the barn. He remembered lying in the grass in the evening after dinner, listening to his grandpa tell stories about the stars of Dragon World. *They were prophecies of what shall be, left by God, to guide the dragons on the right path. They were also the portal between our worlds during times of need. God had separated our worlds, but our destinies were still intertwined.*

Ryan then remembered the last story his grandpa told him about the stars. He said that the time was near for the chosen dragon to be born, and when he was, a star would travel from the heavens and sit upon the precious dragon's egg. He said that the star would then turn into a crystal that would give the young prince the power to travel between our worlds. More stars would fall to be crystals until he was ready to face the last battle, a battle to defeat evil.

Clank! Snarl! Clank!

Ryan was once again startled by a noise coming from the barn. Remembering what his dad had told him about taking care of his grandma and sister, he decided to check it out. He took a deep breath and approached the barn slowly.

Clank! Snarl! Clank!

The noise rang out again! A chill danced down Ryan's spine. There was definitely something in there.

He ignored the voice in his head telling him to run and carefully entered the dark, damp barn. He felt around in front of him for the pull string to the light, but he could not find it. Perhaps it was because he was shaking like dad when he took Isabel to get her drivers permit. *Pull yourself together,* he thought to himself, but he was more than a little scared. He had never been in the barn at night by himself before.

Bam! Ryan stumbled over something hard and fell. "Ouch!" he cried out, and then immediately covered his mouth. S*o much for sneaking up on an intruder.*

He put his hand on the ground to push himself up when the barn began to fill with a soft, red glow. He looked down and saw that it was coming from under his hand. He slowly raised his hand as the glow became brighter and brighter. It was the crystal. *It must have fallen from my pocket.* He stood up and held it out before him. The light grew sharp and seemed to go wherever he needed it to. It was as though it was in sync with his eyes.

He looked around to see what he had tripped over. He knelt to see that it was a plain dark wooden chest. He held the crystal up close and blew away some cobwebs and dust. *I've never seen this before.* Bursting with curiosity, he quickly raised the simple rounded lid.

Inside he saw newspaper clippings, some old pictures, and some clothing. He picked up one of the newspapers and was surprised to see a familiar face; it was that of his great-grandfather! He had the same kind eyes as Grandpa. He looked so young, maybe 20 years old. The headline read: Milton Drakon Saves The Day.

Ryan looked through a few more of the articles, each one describing the heroics of his great-grandpa, Milton. Then Ryan pulled out a soft piece of purple fabric. He stood up and shook it off. It was a jacket. Ryan put in on, it was a little big. He brushed his hands over the smooth soft fabric until his fingers came across a new texture. Ryan removed the jacket and held the crystal up to find that it was a peculiar looking patch. It reminded him of one of his Cub Scout patches. He peered closer and saw that it had a dragon and a man standing back to back with a sword between them. *I've seen this before. It is on the Iron Gate to the driveway. I asked Grandpa about it once and he said that it is the mark of Royal Dragon Warriors.*

Sniff! Snarl! Sniff!

Ryan was surprised by the sound. He had almost forgotten why he was in the barn. He quickly threw the jacket back into the chest and slammed it shut. His ears perked up as he tried to listen for where the noise might be coming from, but all he could hear was the vigorous pounding of his heart.

He cautiously rose to his feet, slowly scanning his surroundings. Snap! He turned in the direction of the noise, but he instantly felt himself being thrown to the ground – and once again covered in wet kisses.

"Tiger!" shouted Ryan with a huge sigh of relief. "What are you doing out here? Come on boy, let's get you back inside." Ryan pushed the mass of black fur and tongue that comprised of Tiger off of him and got back up to his feet. Ryan and Tiger headed back inside.

As Ryan was taking off his muddy boots he noticed his grandma heading up the stairs to go to bed. He wanted to catch her so that he could ask her about the crystal he had found.

Ryan hurried to put his boots away in the closet at the end of the hallway, but as he shut the door he heard something hit the ground. He heard a slight cracking noise coming out from under his foot. He turned and was distressed to see that it was the picture of Grandpa that he had been looking at earlier. He knelt down to pick up the broken glass. *I hope I didn't damage the picture.*

He picked up the picture and noticed that there were some words written on the back. They did not look like any language he had ever seen before.

Ryan cringed as a shrill voice rang out from upstairs. "Get in bed already!" Isabel screeched. "I'm turning out the hall light in two minutes!"

What is she in such a hurry for? Ryan thought as he put all the pieces of the frame onto a small table in the hall. "I suppose she needs all the beauty sleep she can get," he chuckled to himself.

Maybe there is another frame in my closet that will fit this picture. The old wood steps cried out as he raced up the stairs. He nearly tripped, as Isabel had already turned out the hall lights, *thanks for the two minute warning, more like 30 seconds.* He looked toward Grandmas closed door at the end of the hall just in time to see the dim light that was creeping through the cracks around it turn to black. *It has been a long day, I'll tell her about the frame in the morning.*

Ryan placed the picture on his nightstand and hopped into bed. He didn't bother changing into his pajamas; after all, he was on vacation. "Ouch!" Ryan reached into his pocket and pulled out the crystal. He stared at it as he rubbed his now sore leg. There was something so magical about it. Ryan almost seemed to be in a trance as he gazed deeper into it. Sweat began to form on his forehead until it began to drip into his eye. *Oh, that burns!*

He leaned over to his nightstand and grabbed a tissue to wipe his face. He then carefully placed the crystal in the nightstand drawer, "I'll figure you out in the morning," he said softly as he sunk back into the bed. He wiggled around a bit, but he couldn't quite get comfortable. He reached into his other pocket and pulled out the magnifying glass. *Glad I did not fall asleep on that. I don't think grandma would be very happy if I had to tell her that I broke her frame and Grandpa's magnifying glass.* He slid open the nightstand drawer once again and placed the magnifying glass next to the crystal.

As Ryan lay in bed, looking up at the ceiling, he began to think about all the stories Grandpa had told him in that very room. Grandpa always told him amazing tales as he tucked him into bed. Stories of how he had traveled all over the world, our world as well as Dragon World. Ryan's favorite stories were those that portrayed the courageous battles that he had fought with Ashmond to protect our two worlds from colliding and the human race being lost forever to the hunger and greed of Darkness.

Ryan also loved imagining what Dragon World looks like. Grandpa described it as being a beautiful, but mysterious place. It is a place that few had ever seen and even fewer had returned to tell of its beauty. It is a place full of love and honor. It is a place that glorifies God the Father and His amazing love for all creation. Ryan loved to imagine a world where all knew of and worshiped the one true God, but he also loved hearing about the food in Dragon World! Grandpa would tell of legendary feasts and banquets. The queen was known, not only her beauty, but for her cooking as well. "She could make even liver and onions as sweet on the tongue as honey," Grandpa would say. To that Ryan would always jokingly reply, "Isabel can't even make honey as sweet as honey!" Ryan laughed at the thought.

Grandpa also told Ryan all about the royal dragon family and the beautiful castle in which they dwelled. He said that there was nothing like it here. He also warned that Dragon World could also be a very dangerous place. He was referring to Darkness. She is very powerful dragon. She longs to take over our world and use humans as slaves. She hates that humans were made in God's image. She and her followers believe that humans are weak and that Dragons should be revered as Gods by the humans. Grandpa said that for many generations the Drakon family has worked to help the Royal Dragon Family in their crusade to defeat Darkness and keep both worlds safe.

Ryan began to think back to the last story that Grandpa had told him, just before he went missing. It was the one where he had helped Ashmond defeat Darkness. He thought about that story often. At the end of the story Grandpa had said that he had struck a fatal blow to Darkness and that she flew away. It troubled Ryan that her body was never found. He always worried that Dragon World might still be in danger, especially if Grandpa wasn't there to help. *It's just a story*, he would tell himself, but he never could shake that uneasy feeling.

Ryan began to fall asleep. He could almost hear Grandpa's voice whispering through the room. He began to tug at the collar of his shirt as sweat pooled around his neck. The room suddenly seemed very warm, even for a summer evening.

He opened his eyes and let out a heavy sigh, "I can never sleep when it's hot."

He stared at the ceiling for a moment, wishing a fan might magically appear, or maybe just a couple of penguins with buckets of ice cubes. *I wonder if Ellie is still awake.* He learned over to see what time it was, but was distracted by a familiar red glow that was welcoming him from the top drawer of his nightstand.

Ryan turned on the small bedside lamp and tugged on the dresser drawer to find the crystal glowing brighter and brighter, almost like it was calling to him. He picked it up and began to study it once again. There appeared to be something moving inside the crystal. He tried to peer in even closer when he was startled by a blunt tap to his shoulder.

"Ah!" he yelled as he turned and quickly hid the crystal behind his back.

"Calm down jumpy," said Ellie. "It's just me".

"I know," said Ryan as he puffed out his chest. "I was just, umm, trying to, umm, scare you. Yah, that's what I was doing. Did it work?"

Ellie giggled, "No, but you made me laugh?" Ryan had to laugh too. He could not help but smile when he heard Ellie laugh.

"I couldn't sleep, and I saw a light coming from under your door and figured that you couldn't either," replied Ellie as she walked toward the nightstand. "What is that?" She scooped up the picture from the dresser top and studied it intently.

"It's a picture of my grandpa when he was about my age," he answered.

Ellie inspected the picture for a moment more, but was quickly distracted by the red glow that was now flooding the room.

"What's in your hand?"

Ryan told her of the crystal and how he had found it earlier and that he thought it had belonged to his grandpa. They both looked at it, as it began to glow even brighter.

"Wow," said Ellie. "It looks as though something is moving inside of it."

Ryan was surprised, and rather relieved, to know that she could see it too.

Ryan then remembered the magnifying glass. He picked it up and began to examine the crystal closely. Ellie leaned in close to get a better look as well. They stared in disbelief as there appeared to be a tiny black dragon flying inside. It looked just like the one he had seen outside the car window when he arrived!

"Look!" Ellie exclaimed as she pointed to the handle of the magnifying glass as it began to glow as well. All of a sudden the room began to spin… then poof!

Dragon World

"**W**hat just happened?" asked Ellie as she clutched Ryan's arm to steady herself.

"I'm not sure," replied a dizzy Ryan. He waited for his eyes to focus and the spinning to cease, and then he quickly scanned their surroundings.

"We seem to be in some type of forest, but it is like no place I have ever seen before."

The sky was red, and there was a chill in the air. Ryan could not tell if it was twilight or dawn for it didn't seem as though there was a night or day in this land. A soft red glow danced in the distance, encased by a deep crimson. The ground beneath them was cloaked in a thick green moss. The trees were tall and swollen with age, the tops of which were all but consumed by the fiery sky above. Ryan ran his hand over the rough bark of a nearby tree as he took a deep breath, "Do you smell that?" he asked. "It smells like burning leaves."

"I smell it too," replied Ellie as she began to relax her hold on Ryan's arm, for which he was very thankful. She was quite strong.

Ryan closed his eyes and began to breathe slowly. He noticed that, even though he did not know where he was, he felt calm. There was an unmistakable peace within him. He felt strong. He felt confident. For the first time in his life he felt like he was right where he should be. He was home. He began to venture ahead, eager to discover more about this new world, and maybe even about himself.

"Where are you going?" Ellie whispered as she followed close behind him.

Ryan didn't answer; he really didn't even hear her. He just had an overwhelming feeling to keep moving toward something. He just didn't know what.

Soon the dense of the forest began to thin and the two came upon a wide clearing, beyond which laid an amazing new landscape.

"Look," Ellie said as she pointed beyond the clearing. "It's a castle."

They both stood, unable to speak. They just stared in awe.

"It looks like something out of a fairytale," remarked Ellie.

Ryan studied the building for a moment. Then, he looked down at the dragon crystal and magnifying glass in his hands.

"I don't believe it!" he said softly, stunned from his realization.

"What?" asked Ellie as a puzzled expression washed across her face.

"I think I know where we are," he said with a now bubbling enthusiasm. "Follow me!" He fearlessly darted into the clearing. Ellie stood stunned for a moment, then dashed off after him. They soon neared a shimmering moat that seemed to flow with an extraordinary combination of both fire and water. An expansive drawbridge stood tall and firm against the cold stone wall of the castle front.

"Ryan," Ellie huffed, "where do you think we are?"

Ryan stood before the castle, gazing at its magnificent form. His eyes could not even begin to communicate its beauty to his brain.

"Dragon World," he finally answered as a smirk emerged across his face.

"Dragon World," Ellie replied puzzled. "But Dragon World is just a mythical place that your grandpa made up. Ryan, there is no such thing as Dragon World."

Ryan turned to Ellie with an expression of determination that surprised her. "I thought so too," Ryan replied. "But this is just as he described it. Don't you remember the stories, Ellie?"

"Yes, I do, but they were just stories, Ryan," she replied in disbelief. "We can't actually be in Dragon World. Can we?"

"Remember how he would describe the castle," Ryan continued. "Look at it Ellie! It's the same castle. He would also tell us how you could only go to Dragon World if you had the magic portal key and the scale of a Royal dragon."

"Well, yes," Ellie stammered as her eyes widened.

"Look," Ryan said as he pulled the dragon crystal and the magnifying glass from his pocket for her to see. "The crystal must be the portal key and the handle of the magnifying glass must from a royal dragon. That's why they were glowing. They were calling us here!"

Ellie was looking at Ryan with skepticism when they noticed a swishing sound coming from above their heads. They slowly looked up only to see a very purple and very plump, little dragon flying overhead.

"You've got to be kidding," Ellie said under her breath.

"Do you believe me now?" Ryan asked with an even bigger smirk. It wasn't often that he was right when it came to arguments with Ellie!

The plump purple dragon suddenly began to shriek, very loudly! Ryan and Ellie covered their ears, but there was no escaping the shrill screeches. Suddenly the ground beneath them began to tremble. They turned to see the massive drawbridge barreling toward the earth before them. The plump purple dragon promptly flew back behind the safety of the castle walls.

Ryan dropped his hands from his ears as his attention was now focused on the descent of the drawbridge. It was incredible. It looked to be the size of a football field and the chains that held it were larger than a school bus. It appeared to be made of wood, but it shimmered with a rainbow of colors like nothing he had ever seen before.

Ellie quickly grabbed Ryan and pulled him out of the way. Thud! It landed with great force and caused dust to rise into the heavens above. As it cleared they began to make out the figure of another dragon that was swiftly approaching them from within the castle walls.

"Welcome," announced a booming voice. "We have been waiting for you. Come, join the celebration."

"You have?" asked Ellie as they both began to get up and dust themselves off. The dust sparkled, reminding Ellie of fairy dust.

"Who are you?" asked Ryan with a surprising amount of power.

"I am Capula, keeper of the gate." the figure replied as though he had a chip on his shoulder. "The Royal Family is expecting you."

As the dust settled completely Ryan and Ellie saw a very large olive-green dragon standing before them. His color was as drab as his temperament. He was wearing a purple uniform with a symbol on the chest. Ryan immediately recognized the design. It was the crest of the Dragon Warriors!

Ryan and Ellie followed Capula, as he turned and led them over the bridge and into the depths of the massive castle.

The grandeur of the castle foyer exuded unimaginable beauty. The walls were smooth like glass and embraced grand portraits and paintings. Ryan felt at ease, as they reminded him of the pictures in Grandma's house. Though here he felt more like a mouse, due to the sheer scale of his surroundings. They glanced at the paintings as they were lead down the vast grand hall at the end of which stood two heavy ornate doors.

Suddenly, Ellie began to tug excessively at Ryan's shirt, "Look!" she exclaimed in a hushed tone! Ryan stopped and stared in awe. He could not believe his eyes! On the wall hung a painting of Grandpa! He was holding a sword and next to him stood a massive dragon. Ryan approached the painting and ran his fingers across the eyes of the Dragon.

"Ashmond," Ryan said softly.

He knew it was him. He looked just as Grandpa had described. The yellow of his scales shimmered as gold on a bright summer's day. Green encased his blazing blue eyes and reappeared at the very tip of his long muscular tail. His eyes were magnificent. Ryan knew they would be. They were sharp and forceful, yet they had a gentle grace that was unmistakable.

Just when Ryan and Ellie had thought the castle could not possibly hold anymore beauty and surprise, the doors at the end of the hall parted, welcoming them to untold wonders.

"Come," ordered the booming voice of Capula. "Your presence is required post haste."

The Explanation

Mere words could not describe the lavish splendor that befell the vast throne chamber before them. It radiated with grace and allure. Fierce stone walls stood strong and proud while massive stone pillars seemed to disappear into the heavens above. The powerful room embraced robust statues, depicting grand dragon warriors and opulent portraits adorned the walls. A gold trimmed deep-purple pathway was flanked on either side by royal dragon soldiers, the number of which was matched only by their evident strength. Each one was draped in purple and proudly bared the crest of the Royal dragon family.

"This can't be real," Ellie whispered to Ryan.

He took no notice of her remark. His mind was fixated on what lie ahead. The path before him cried like a rapid waterfall, drowning out all of creation. The cries crashed upon him, ushering him forward.

Ellie grabbed his hand as he pursued the path, like a moth to flame. They soon reached the end of the line and stopped as the roar of a trumpet saturated the room.

"Announcing Ryan and Ellie, protectors to the Royal Dragon Family," boomed Capula.

Ryan snapped back to his senses, he felt as though he was caught in the world between dreams and reality. Before them stood two striking dragons. Their identity was unmistakable. It was King Ashmond and Queen Hadoss.

The Queen was breathtaking. She was cloaked in soft violet scales that shimmered like crystals flooded with sunlight. Blue and teal danced around her soft purple eyes and reemerged down her long flowing tail. Ryan felt drawn into her soft pale purple Irises. As he gazed into them he sensed a sadness within her that carried an obvious weight deep within her soul. He looked down to see her long majestic talons clutching a stunning golden egg. It sparkled like a beautiful sunrise over crystal clear waters.

"We are honored that you have joined us," said Ashmond, "Your grandma said that she would get you to us in time, though we had expected that she would have joined you"

"Grandma?" Ryan asked with a puzzled tone.

The queen looked over to her powerful husband, "It appears that Ryan has found his way on his own. His spirit link must be strong to have heard our call."

Ashmond approached Ryan and Ellie, "All will be explained," he charged. "First, let us eat."

Ryan and Ellie were led by a tall thin green dragon, wearing a rather funny little hat, into a grand banquet room. They were seated across from each other. Ryan placed his napkin into his lap and gave Ellie a reassuring smile.

The king and queen joined them at the table. Soon Ryan and Ellie noticed enchanting aromas consuming the room. The food being placed upon the table was glorious! All of their favorites were there. It was like Christmas, Thanksgiving and Easter all rolled into one opulent meal!

"This must be what Heaven smells like," joked Ryan to Ellie.

"Please, Enjoy," said the queen softly as she passed the golden egg off to a short, plump yellow little dragon in what slightly resembled a nurse's uniform.

Ryan leaned forward to help himself when a very tiny blue dragon, about the size of a squirrel, appeared before him. "Please, allow me sir," hissed the little dragon as he scurried across the table to fill Ryan's plate with food.

Ryan smiled over at Ellie as another small blue dragon appeared and began to serve her as well. It was rather comical the way they could balance the plates on their table as they filled them full of food. It was almost acrobatic, like a little circus performance.

They both thanked the queen and began to eat.

This definitely beats Isabel's cooking, Ryan thought to himself.

As Ryan finished his first helping of what was the best sweet potato soufflé he had ever tasted, he noticed that there was something familiar about his plate. He gently used his napkin to clear the plate.

"This is the same china set that my grandma has," announced Ryan rather loudly, startling Ellie and the queen.

"Why, yes it is," replied the queen as she composed herself. "I had a set made especially for her. She had always admired mine."

Ryan, surprised by her reply, sternly asked, "How do you know my grandma and how is she to thank for bringing us to you?"

Ashmond answered for his wife, "We have known your family for many generations. Your ancestors have proven to be great protectors of Dragon World for as far back as our history can be told. Your grandparents have traveled here many times."

"I thought that Dragon World was just a place in a story that my grandpa made up." Ryan felt as though all that he had ever known needed to be questioned.

The Queen then signaled for the table to be cleared, along with the room. Ryan, being a growing boy, quickly shoveled a few last bites into his mouth. After all, he didn't want a growling in his tummy to distract him from getting answers.

Ashmond continued once the room was cleared, "Your grandpa started coming here when he was about your age, I was just an egg. He would come with his grandfather, your great-grandfather Milton

Drakon, to visit my father. They were very close. Back then there was peace though out the land. Eventually, as time went on, and we grew older, your grandpa began to court your grandma, around the same time that I began to court my beautiful bride." Ashmond looked over to the queen; a look of admiration graced both their faces. Ryan saw that same look exchanged between his grandparents often.

"Courted?" asked Ryan with a puzzled face.

"Yes," replied Ashmond, "your grandparents grew up together, as friends, not unlike you and Ellie." Ellie blushed slightly as Ryan glanced across the table at her. "As they grew, so did their feelings for one another. Your grandpa James knew he would one day have Ruth as his bride. He made his intentions of marriage know to her father and began to court her. It was then that he brought her to Dragon World, and she found out that the stories she had grown up listening to, alongside your grandpa, were true."

Ryan felt his lips curl to a smile. He knew just how his grandpa felt.

"Eventually they married," continued Ashmond, "The ceremony was right here in this very hall. It was a grand event. Our entire kingdom came out to celebrate with us. Our families have been blessed with many happy celebrations over the years, but sadly, they have become fewer and fewer through the ages.

"Why? Asked Ellie.

Ashmond's might seem to melt as snow pressed beneath the relenting heat of the sun. His powerful presence evaporated, exposing the scars of cold harsh battles. "A dark prophecy came to be known throughout all the land that a formidable evil would rise from the depths of our world bringing about great suffering and fear. Many would be lost, some by the sword, but more to the misguided allure of immorality and false free will. My father and your great-grandfather vowed to defeat this great evil. Soon she appeared, known only by the name of Darkness."

Ryan gasped. He had heard this name many times before in Grandpas stories. Darkness. It rang out like the shrill cries of death itself. Ryan looked over at Ellie, her enchanting face was now as pale as her fair blonde hair. Ashmond went on, "Soon soldiers were training as battles began to be fought. The kingdom was divided. There were those that chose to side with Darkness as she promised to enslave the human race and make her followers gods."

Ryan looked painfully across the table to Ellie. He could see that she had finally come to realize that this was not all some crazy dream. He too was beginning to feel the weight of the call to war. He quietly rose from his chair, rounded the long ornate table and sat down beside her. Ellie was not one to wear her heart on her sleeve, but she would have moments when her soul longed for her mother. She never spoke of them, but Ryan could see the pain in her eyes. Normally, he would try to make her laugh to relieve her anxiety, but he used his better judgment and decided that this was probably not the best time to hold dinner rolls to the side of his head and begin to prance around like a space princess, although that was one of Ellie's favorite bits.

The Queen leaned in close to Ashmond. "Look," she whispered softly, "He is just like James, ever the protector."

Ryan felt proud to be compared to Grandpa, though he still viewed himself as more of a clown than a protector.

Ashmond continued on, "The battle raged for many years, eventually claiming the life of my father and of your great-grandfather, suddenly making their fight ours."

"Grandpa and I fought many battles together and soon it seemed to come down to one very important night. No longer was Dragon World equally divided. Most had come to see the true wickedness of

Darkness. Many had abandoned her and joined our fight. She decided to make one last attempt to destroy our world, but your grandpa put a stop to her once and for all, well, that is what we thought anyways."

Ashmond then went on to tell about the last visit that they had received from Grandpa and Grandma. It was just after the Queen had delivered the royal egg. Grandpa and Grandma had returned to visit with the king and queen to congratulate them and to make plans to bring Ryan for his first visit. It was decided that a party would be thrown to introduce the new prince, and Ryan, the next dragon warrior.

There was peace throughout the kingdom, thanks to Grandpa for having defeated Darkness. The queen was delighted to know that her son would grow up in a world without war, especially since it had been prophesied that the evil one would kidnap a dragon of the royal bloodline and raise him to become a powerful soldier of evil.

After we had shared a meal our dear friends were ready to say goodnight. Grandpa went into the nursery, where the royal egg was, to say a good night prayer of protection over the slumbering prince. The king, queen, and Grandma waited in the hall outside the nursery for Grandpa to join them. Suddenly, they heard a loud crash. As the nursery doors flew open, they were shocked to see an unwelcomed face. It was Darkness! She had returned!

"Take the prince to safety!" shouted Grandpa as he used a floor lamp to fend off Darkness. I hastily tucked my son inside my wing and rushed him to the queen.

I ordered the women to safety, but, when I rushed back into the nursery to aid Grandpa in the battle, but I saw that I was too late. I came just in time to see Darkness flying off into the night carrying Grandpa in her claws. He saw a message burned into the wall. It read:

Follow me and the old man dies

I fell to the ground in anguish. I was thankful that Grandpa had saved my son, but I was saddened that it came at such a high price.

Later I met with the knights of the Dragon Court and the decision was made that the Prince needed to be hidden away from Darkness. He must be kept safe at all costs. We could not allow the prophecy to come true. We must keep the prince safe, or Dragon World, as we know it, would cease to exist as and the human would be next!

Ellie held Ryan's hand and looked into his eyes. Ryan was trying to be brave, but the pain of his breaking heart was radiating through his whole body.

DESTINY UNFOLDS

The king and queen escorted Ryan and Ellie to the gardens outside to give Ryan some time to absorb what he had learned before Ashmond finished the story.

The flowers in the garden were beautiful. They were large and quite unique, like most everything in Dragon World. Some stood as tall as trees, gulping in the warmth of the blood red sun, while others crept along the ground as ants to a picnic basket, fighting for enough sweet life-giving warmth to substance them.

Ryan walked on with the king as Ellie and Queen paused to study the beauty that God had laid before them.

Ellie stopped when a particularly bright-blue flower captured her eye. It flowed as running water and shimmered like gathered stars from the heavens. She knelt down near it as its gentle aroma danced in a soft breeze like a ballerina across a stage. Its perfume was one of a thousand forgotten memories. It reminded her of her cat, Otis, then of the time her father took her to a baseball game and finally of her mother twirling her around the living room and singing to her. Tears began to well up in her eyes at the sweet vivid memory of her mother.

"That is a very special flower," the queen said gently as she approached Ellie. "We call it shuv-zachar. It means turn back memory in Hebrew. They are very unique in that they possess the extraordinary power to bring forth blessed memories of the past. You may take one if you like."

Ellie thanked the queen and plucked one of the smaller buds from the plant. She tucked the flower in her hair, fastening it securely under her red ribbon.

Ryan was much too eager for answers to take such simple pleasure in the flowers of the garden. "What happened to my grandpa?" he asked Ashmond in a sharp determined tone as he planted his feet firmly on the ground. "I will not take another step until you tell me what Darkness has done with him?"

Ashmond looked upon Ryan's troubled face with sorrow. "We believe she is holding him captive," he replied sadly.

"Why?" Ryan asked in a sort of panic, yet relieved to know that Grandpa may still be alive.

"Only a dragon warrior can release the prince from his egg and train him. We believe that she plans to kidnap the prince and force your grandpa to train him to serve her evil desires."

Ryan knew that his grandpa would never do such a thing. He would die first. Ryan looked to the ground and shook his head. Anxiety dominated him once again. "We have sent soldiers to retrieve him, but her fortress is strong," continued Ashmond. "We have also captured spies that Darkness has sent into the kingdom and they are much more willing to talk than I believe your grandpa ever would be." He stood tall to express his admiration for Grandpa's strong character and resolve.

"Yes," replied Ryan, wanting to honor his Grandpa more than ever. "How can I help?"

Ashmond turned to Queen Hadoss and gently took the golden egg from her. Ryan noticed as a single tear swelled within her eye, trickling down her teal and purple scales as the precious egg left the loving embrace of her strong talons.

"You must protect the prince," he replied as he placed the egg into Ryan's arms. "It is up to you to get him back to your world and train him to defeat Darkness."

Ryan looked at the egg as fears plagued his every thought "What about Grandpa?" he asked, unable to escape the torment of his uncertainty. "We can't just leave him there, alone, with that monster!"

Ashmond replied sternly. He knew Ryan's pain. This was not easy for anyone. "We have a plan in place to save him," assured Ashmond. "You must trust us just as we trust you with our most precious possession." Ashmond ran his talon gently over the golden egg shell. "You must make sure the prince is safe before I can send my best soldiers to raid her fortress."

Ryan was still very troubled about his Grandpa, but he understood that he alone could not save Grandpa, and the soldiers could not save Grandpa and guard the egg at the same time.

"It's time for the prince to be called from his egg," continued Ashmond with a sense of urgency. "You must release him and begin his training."

Ryan looked at the golden egg. He was frightened at the thought of such responsibility, but he thought about his grandpa. He then looked up at the queen. He knew this must be the hardest thing she had ever done. If she could be brave enough to trust an eleven year old boy with her one and only son, then he must trust Grandpa to the hands of a fleet of Dragon Soldiers, especially since they genuinely loved him about as much as Ryan did.

"I will give my life to serve Dragon World," Ryan said, as he looked straight at the queen. "I will protect the prince with my life."

As his gaze fell deep into her beautiful eyes, a sense of love and admiration filled him. He felt slightly shocked at the realization that he actually meant those heavy words.

"Thank you," she replied as she lowered her head and swung her tail around her, as to brace herself from the pain that was rising within her.

Ryan knew that trusting him with her only son must not be easy, mom hardly trusted him with a house key, let alone the only prophesized savior of an ancient dragon world that was threatened to be destroyed by pure evil!

Ryan thought for a moment, and then turned his attention to Ashmond as he was comforting his wife, "One more thing, how am I to hide a Dragon in my world? People are bound to notice him," questioned Ryan.

"In your world he will only be visible to those that have touched the soil of Dragon World."

"There are others that have traveled here?" asked Ellie.

"Yes," replied Ashmond as he looked at Ellie. Her sweet face seemingly relieved to know that they might not be alone in this venture. "Just as your world has many different countries, so does ours. Every land has rulers and those that seek to destroy them in the name of the evil known as Darkness. Therefore, they too are in need of protectors from your world."

Ellie looked over to Ryan, "I bet you would pay attention in that History class," she replied knowing that he hated History class.

"Just be warned," Ashmond's gaze grew intense then fell upon Ryan, penetrating him to his very soul. "The battle of good and evil is not just an external battle. Keep yourselves in prayer. Turn to God for guidance in all that you do. Keep yourselves dedicated to the Lord and He will bless your journey. We have faith that we will win this battle. We know that we stand at an advantage in that we do not lean on our own understanding or strength. We know that all that we have comes from the one true God. Darkness longs to sit in his throne, but we know that evil will not prevail; for all those that allow evil to engulf their souls shall fall and be lost for all eternity."

Ashmond then signaled for the tall thin dragon in the funny hat to come. "This is the book of Dragon history," said Ashmond as he freed a small book from a silky piece of golden cloth. "It contains all that you will need to know in order to train and care for the young prince. It also includes a list of other protectors that may help you along the way."

Ashmond then leaned down and handed it to Ellie. "You must protect this book." he continued as he smiled at Ellie. "Ryan will need you, just as his grandpa needed his grandma. A protector cannot complete his task alone."

Ellie took the book. "I will," she replied as she ran her fingers over the dark green cover. It looked to be made of aged leather, it felt remarkably smooth, her finger glided across it like silk across a piece of glass. It was simple looking, especially for the secrets it held.

Ashmond looked deep into Ellie's eye, his tone grew intense, "Just know that Darkness would do anything to get her talons on this book. If she were to have it not only would she know the secrets of the Royal Family, but she would also know the location of all the protectors throughout your world. Our defenses would surely perish as dust in the wind."

Ashmond's piercing blue eyes fell upon Ryan, "Once you return home you must say the name of the young prince in order to awaken him," instructed Ashmond.

"Sounds simple enough," replied Ryan. "What is his name?"

"It is within you to choose his name," answered Ashmond.

"Me?" Ryan said sheepishly.

Ryan looked down at the golden egg in awe. The responsibility before him sat in his stomach like a lead sandwich.

"Ryan," continued Ashmond. "Once you have returned home, you must repeat your family crest to open the book. Our elders have charmed it so that it will only open when you say those words."

Ryan knew his families crest well. His grandpa had taught him from a very young age. His grandpa had it engraved on the inside of his wedding band. He showed it to Ryan once. It read,

Semper in umbris, Fraternitas aeternus

In English, his crest meant forever in the shadows, forever brothers. Ryan never understood what it meant until now. Dragon World was parallel to ours, as if in the shadows, and our families' fellowship as brothers.

An elusive smile skimmed Ryan's face, quickly fading with the realization that his grandfather's ring may mean that Darkness holds more cards then they had thought. He turned to Ashmond in angst. "Is it possible that Darkness knows that she needs the crest to open the book?" questioned Ryan in a panic.

"I suppose it is possible that a spy may have found out that information and gotten it to her, that's why you must take the prince and book to safety right away!" replied Ashmond.

Ryan knew that if Darkness found the inscription of Grandpa's ring all might be lost! "The prince may be in more danger than we thought," he cried out. "Darkness may already have the family crest!"

Ryan began to explain when a sudden flash of light exploded near the castle gates, causing the earth beneath them began to tremble and shake. Ashmond let out a mighty roar as a group of soldiers surrounded them. "Hurry we must get you to safety, the castle is under attack!"

Prophecy Lies Ahead

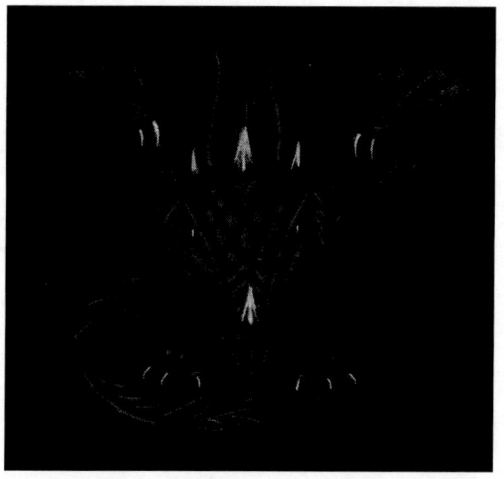

The soldiers ushered Ryan and Ellie to a tunnel beneath the castle walls. "You will be safe in here," yelled a soldier as his face disappeared behind heavy-laden doors. The sound of the lock caused their blood to curdle like milk left in the summer sun. It echoed through the caves, soon leaving them with only the muffled cries of battle waging in the royal gardens.

"Ryan?" asked Ellie in a timid voice.

"I'm here," he replied even more timidly.

"I can't see a thing," Ellie said as he felt her reach for his arm.

As their hands met, Ryan felt his warmth and strength return to him. Her soft slender fingers melted into his. His soul felt as though it was glowing. He looked down to see that it was not his soul at all, but the crystal that was in his pocket! He quickly grabbed it as the soft red glow illuminated their tomb like surroundings. *I am not sure that being able to see is making me feel any better,* thought Ryan as he shuttered at the eerie crept like stone walls. *This feels more like a final resting place, than a safe haven.* Ryan tucked the egg away safely inside his shirt as Ellie began to study their surroundings and venture deeper in the cave, forcing Ryan to follow.

Soon they came upon intricate drawings on the stark gray cave walls.

"Look," said Ellie, now surprisingly calm, "this drawing, it looks just like you."

Ryan took a closer look. It did look like him! He was clutching a sword while riding on the back of a black dragon. There were a whole line of drawings; it was as if they were telling a story. They followed the drawings down the cave walls. They saw drawings of Grandpa and Grandma with a crystal similar to the one Ryan held.

"This must be the prophecy wall. Grandpa mentioned this in some of his stories," Ryan said softly as he ran his fingers over an image of his grandpa.

Ellie tugged on Ryan's arm. "Look!" she exclaimed as she nearly pulled him over.

Ryan was amazed to see a large drawing of five crystals. They were not on the walls like the others. They were on what appeared to be a raised part of the cave floor, almost like a table. It was in the center of the cave. The ceiling above seemed to rise endlessly.

"This one matches the crystal in your hand," Ellie continued as she pointed to the drawing. Her words softly echoed as they bounced around the opening above.

Ryan noticed that there were words written around each of the crystals.

"I wonder what language this is," Ellie questioned as she ran her hand over them. "Ouch! They are hot!" she exclaimed as she blew on her fingers.

Ryan leaned in closer to get a better look. "I've seen these words before. Quick, do you still have that picture of my grandpa that was on my nightstand?"

Ellie reached into her pocket, "I do!" She carefully set down the book that Ashmond had entrusted to her and pulled the picture from her pocket.

They quickly flipped it over and looked at the words. They look like the same language

"I wonder what it means," Said Ellie.

Ryan moved the crystal over the letters to get a better look when suddenly the letters began to jump around! They soon spelled out a mysterious message…

> Salvation lies within the one born black as sin, yet beats with a heart as white as snow.

"What do you think that means?" Ellie asked Ryan as she placed the picture back into her pocket.

"I'm not sure." Ryan began to think back to the stories that his grandpa had told him. He wondered if there might be a clue within the stories.

All at once, the ground began to tremble and the letters vanished as quickly as they had appeared. They then heard what sounded like the Earth itself crying out for mercy. They quickly looked toward the entrance of the tunnel only to see fire and smoke ravishing every inch. They then heard muffled voices shouting. Suddenly a burly voice rang out. At first it was hard to understand, but it quickly became very clear, three urgent letters, "Run!"

"Darkness must have taken the castle, we must get the prince home," shouted Ryan to Ellie as they ran deep into the caves.

"But how?" asked a slightly winded Ellie, "How do we get home?" Ryan's feet suddenly turned to lead weights as the paralyzing realization that he didn't have a clue overcame him!

Fire chased their heels as they continued to move deeper and deeper into the cave until it finally reached its limit. They slowed as they came upon an ornate looking door, similar those of the throne room.

"It's our only way out" said Ryan as he grabbed Ellie's hand and urged her toward the door.

"Wait!" Ellie cried, pulling against him. "The book! I set in down when we were looking at the drawings. It's still in the cave!"

Ryan looked at Ellie. She looked so scared. He had never really seen her so scared before. She was usually so brave and pulled together. Usually, she was holding him together, though he would never admit it aloud.

Ryan looked down toward the golden egg that was cradling the young prince, then back at the door. He knew it was crucial to get the prince to safety, and he wanted to get to safety too, but he also knew that they must not let Darkness get that book.

"Ellie," he ordered bravely as he offered the egg to her, "take the prince and hide. I will go and get the book."

"No Ryan," she asserted. "The book is my responsibility. I will go and retrieve it."

Ryan, knowing that he would never win this argument reluctantly tucked the golden egg back inside his shirt and took her by the hand again, "We will do this together then."

A smile flashed across Ellie's soiled face.

Ryan really like the way she looked at him. He liked the way he felt in Dragon World. Even with all that was going on, he felt strong. He knew what must be done and just how to do it.

They carefully scurried back through the tunnel. The sounds of intense battle grew louder with every step they took. They soon found themselves surrounded by thick black smoke. Ryan began to cough. Ellie pulled him to the ground and handed him a piece of cloth that she had torn from her shirt in which to cover his mouth.

"We are close," Ellie said softly. "I left it right over there." She pointed toward the source of the smoke.

Great, thought Ryan, *that's just where we shouldn't be!*

They began to inch closer toward where the book should be. Ryan noticed that the sounds of battle seemed to have disappeared.

"There it is," she whispered.

Without warning, an intense torrent of fire and smoke filled the tunnel before them. The smoke cleared, revealing a sickening collection of fallen dragon soldiers.

THE FIRST ENCOUNTER

he cave grew dark as the surrounding fires relented. The deafening silence almost made Ryan long for the cries of battle to return.

"Do you think it's safe?" Ellie asked in a hushed whisper.

"There's only one way to find out," Ryan boasted, putting on his best brave face. "Let's get the book." *And get out of here!*

They reluctantly began to creep away from the wall of the cave, relying heavily on their hands to guide them across the blackened scorched floor, as expiring flames quickly began to flicker and die. Ryan stopped as suddenly as a bug on a windshield.

"What is it?" Ellie whispered.

"I think I feel something," he replied as he carefully moved his hand over an odd rough surface.

"Is it the book?" asked Ellie a little louder.

"I'm not sure," replied Ryan, "I wish I could see."

All at once, his wish was answered as the cave filled with the hot red glow of fire. Ryan and Ellie dug their faces into the dirt, shielding their faces from the unrelenting heat.

Ryan looked up and gasped in horror to see that is hand was not on the book, but grasping a spiky red tail! He looked around, the cave now brightly lit, once again exposing the devastation surrounding them. Dragon soldiers lay wounded and unresponsive, leading Ryan to the harsh realization that the dragon soldiers may have not won this battle. The thought filled him with despair as he went on to realize that they were then on their own and alone with the enemy!

"Run!" Ryan shouted to Ellie. He quickly pulled out the crystal and egg and handed them to her. "Go, save the prince!"

Ryan turned back toward his wicked opponent and prepared to face battle. He looked up in horror as eyes as black as death glared down at him. He felt a chill run screaming down his spine. Her scales moved like flowing lava. Her muscular presence resonated with hate and resentment. All the stories his grandpa had told him sprinted through his mind. He quickly scanned the cave for some way out. Salvation stood just a few feet from him, in the form of a sword wedged into the ground.

"So," hissed the lava red dragon. "You must be the chosen dragon warrior. You do not look like much."

Ryan began to move stealthily toward the sword as he replied to the beast before him. "You know who I am, but I have yet to discover who you are."

"Who am I?" she replied with contempt. "You ignorant little fool, I am Darkness, great and powerful ruler of this world."

Ryan shuddered at the sound of her name, the very word seemed to pierce his soul. "You are?" he replied, trying to hide the fear in his voice. "I thought Ashmond was ruler."

Ryan covered his ears as Darkness let out a great cry that melted into a heckling laugh, "That fool? His time has come to step aside. I shall tear the veil that separates our worlds and rule all that live. I shall be worshipped by all that inhabit the Earth!"

"I don't think so!" shouted Ryan as he lunged for the sword and pointed it firmly at the heart of his enemy.

Ryan felt the ground tremble as Darkness began to laugh once again, "Perhaps there is a bit of dragon warrior in you yet," she scoffed.

"Return my grandpa!" Ryan shouted with all the courage he could muster. "Or else!"

"You may have courage," she laughed. "But you have no chance of defeating me young warrior."

Darkness then let out a large bellow of smoke. Ryan began to cough and lost sight of her as it engulfed his eyes. He tried to see past the stinging tears that were now rapidly forming. He plunged the sword at a large shape, only to find it to be a cold hard stone. He tried again and again, but he could not find his intended target. Suddenly sound rang out like thunder all around him as he felt heat poor down upon his neck. He turned and raised his sword just as a thin stream of fire streamed upon him. "Ouch!" he cried as he dropped the quickly melting sword.

Darkness gave out a great cackle, as she watched him frantically blow on his severely burnt fingers.

Her laugh did not last though, as she quickly grew impatient, "Enough with these games, I shall give you one last chance young warrior. You know what I have come for. Tell me, where is the prince?"

Ryan, overwhelmed by his inevitable demise, looked franticly around the room. *This can't be it? Grandpa would find a way out of this and so must I!*

Darkness slithered toward Ryan and twisted her long neck until her dark as death eyes were equal with his, "Come child, don't make the same mistakes as your forefathers. Give the prince to me and together we will be rich with power! I can give you so much more than Ashmond ever could."

The small patches of fire around them, now nearly extinguished, were giving off little light. As the tears withdrew, Ryan could barely make out a lurking behind Darkness. The shadowy form slowly approached, and Ryan was relieved as he recognized the funny hat upon its head. It was the king's servant, but he looked desperately wounded.

Ryan called upon all the strength his body had left as he puffed out his chest and replied with honor, "I have made my choice Darkness. I vow to protect Dragon World and the Royal Family. I choose the righteous path that my ancestors have set before me. I am proud to be a Dragon Warrior! I am proud to serve all that is good, and destroy all that is evil!"

Infuriated with his arrogance, Darkness filled with rage, "Then I shall tell your grandpa goodbye for you," she snarled as she began to fill with fire once again. Ryan stood in fear, unable to move.

"Catch!" shouted the familiar form as he tossed a shield to Ryan just before collapsing to the cold stone ground.

Ryan caught the shield, to his own amazement, and quickly held it up just as a torrent of fire rained down on him. He fell to one knee under the surmounting pressure of the fire. It seemed endless. Ryan could not hold on much longer. The shield began to glow under the heat and pressure. Ryan could feel sweat pouring from his face. The heat was agonizing. He began to pray to God for help.

"Hold on Ryan," the sound of Ellie's voice flowed through the air like a welcomed breeze on a hot July day. She pulled the crystal from her pocket and the ribbon from her hair. She quickly wrapped the ribbon around the crystal and began to swing it over her head, she then slingshot the crystal right toward Darkness! Ryan watched as the crystal headed right for her, but Ellie missed! It hit the rocks just above Darkness. Ryan, now very weak, fell to the ground.

He found slight relief on the cold rock floor. He began to loosen his grip on the shield. Suddenly he heard a noise, like horses running on an old brick road. He forced himself to regain his grip. He was relieved as the relentless stream of fire quickly ceased. In a daze, Ryan could just make out Ellie's cries.

"Run!"

Ryan looked up to see an avalanche of rocks coming toward him. He then felt a swift tug on his shirt, yanking him to his feet. It was Ellie! She had not missed her intended target, Ryan had however misjudged just what that target was!

The rocks began to tumble upon the shield as they ran as fast as they could toward the entrance to the cave. Ryan was relying heavily on Ellie, as he was still rather dazed.

"There!" yelled Ellie as she pulled a very weak Ryan toward a small depression along the cave wall, close to the entrance. They pressed themselves against the stone. Ryan, his wits quickly returning as the cool cave wall brought much needed relief, held the shield up to block them from the heavy shower of passing rocks and dirt.

Suddenly all was quiet… and very dark.

Triumphant Return

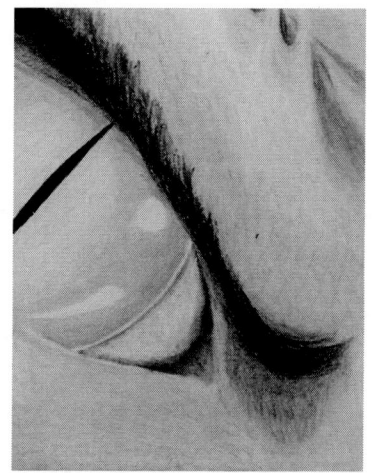

"Ryan," whispered Ellie, "are you okay?"

"Yes," he replied weakly, "I think so." His body was now numb with pain. "I can't believe you came back for me," He moaned as he clutched his very sore ribs.

"Modest much?" joked Ellie. "I came back for the book, after all, and it is my responsibility."

Ryan smiled. He loved that even now Ellie had a sense of humor. "Now, how are we going to find our way out of here?" asked Ryan, as he pushed against the once redeeming rocks that were now barricading them from freedom.

"Do I have to think of everything?" Ellie joked, though not as spirited as before.

They both began to blink, desperately trying to get their eyes to discern their surroundings in the darkness encasing them.

"Can you see anything?" asked Ellie.

"No," replied Ryan. "Wait!"

Ryan rubbed his eyes. I think I see a light. He carefully moved toward the faint red glow. He could feel the ground become uneven as he stepped onto small rocks and pebbles. As he approached, he felt the ground become warm. He knelt down and began to wipe away stones and dirt with his hands, the light becoming ever brighter, until he recognized its source. It was the crystal! He held it up as it began to glow even brighter, illuminating their new prison.

Ellie sighed with relief at the sight of the crystal. "That is one glorious crystal!"

They looked around in despair. Large boulders, stones and dirt barricaded the entrance to the cave.

"Well," said Ryan. "At least we know of another way out. Let's go."

Ryan took Ellie by the hand and began to lead the way deeper into the cave.

"Wait!" Ellie exclaimed. "We cannot leave without the book!"

Ryan, not as eager as he was once to retrieve the book, knew that she was right. The two retraced their steps and began to seek its precious pages from within the depths of seemingly endless hoard of stones and debris.

"Oh," cried a dirt covered Ellie, "How will we ever find that book in all this mess?"

Ryan hated to see her so distressed. "Don't worry Ellie," he said as he took her by the hand. "If there was one thing that Grandpa's stories have taught me, it's that the good guys always win." Ryan then handed Ellie the flower she had picked from the garden. She had dropped it when she removed the ribbon from her hair. Ryan had just come across it while looking for the book.

Ellie smiled at Ryan. Deep cuts and burns bled out from behind the mask of dirt that cloaked his face.

Suddenly the unwelcomed sound of thunder barreled through the cave walls, causing the ground beneath them to tremble.

"What was that?" asked an alarmed Ellie.

"I don't know," replied Ryan, as he turned, "I think it came from over there."

They slowly began to walk deeper into the cave. Unsure if the source of the noise was friend or foe.

"Maybe it is Ashmond," said Ellie, encouraged by Ryan's earlier words about the good guys always winning. "Maybe he has come to save us."

Again, the noise crawled through the stale thin air.

Ryan held the crystal up high trying to ward off any surprises from the dark surrounding them.

"Look!" Ellie shouted as she pointed straight out in front of them. "It's the book!"

Ellie and Ryan darted forward, trying desperately not to trip on all the loose stones that blanketed the cave floor. Ellie knelt down to scoop up the book.

"It's stuck," she grunted as she tugged at it.

"Here, let me try," replied Ryan as he passed the crystal to Ellie.

Ryan gave a few good tugs, but it was really stuck! He motioned for Ellie to bring the light closer so that he could get a better look. They both frantically began to remove stones from around the book when they once again heard the sound of thunder cry out. It sounded as though they were right on top of the source. They could feel the ground moving beneath them.

"Look," said Ellie in a frightened voice.

There sat the book, free of stones and debris, but captive to something much worse; the vile large, red talons of Darkness!

Smells Like Danger

llie held her hand over her mouth as she gasped.

"Is she dead?" asked Ellie.

"I'm not sure," replied Ryan. "Let's not wait around to find out!"

Ryan placed one hand securely around the book and while the other gradually lifted the large red claws that lay limp upon the book.

"Almost got it," he said as he gently pulled the book to freedom.

The deafening boom of thunder caused the ground to tremble and cry out as rocks began to shift and sway as leaves on a tree, bowing to the wind.

Ryan grabbed his shield to protect them from the onset of rocks and debris.

Soon the cave grew quiet and still once more.

"I don't think it is safe for us to stay in here," said Ellie between coughs.

"I agree," said Ryan as he handed the book to Ellie. "Let's get out of here!"

Ellie led the way, holding the crystal up high. They headed straight toward the ornate door where Ryan had left Ellie earlier. Ryan began to notice that the cave had many little smaller passages. Some were no larger than a mouse hole while some were quite large. He was surprised as he saw Ellie turned off the main path and head inside one of the lesser passages.

"Where are you going? He asked somewhat frantically. "Let's just get out of here!"

Ellie did not reply. Ryan had no choice but to follow her.

They had to crawl on their hands and knees to enter the tunnel. "Why are we going in here?" said Ryan in a hurried tenor, "We are only a short distance from getting out of here. We need to get the prince, *and ourselves*, to safety." As Ryan finished his sentence it dawned on him, *where was the prince?* He began to feel a sense of panic come over him.

"Wait!" Ryan yelled to Ellie in a panic, "What did you do with the egg?"

Ellie, now digging in the dirt, "Don't worry," she said as she pulled an object from the cave floor. "He is right here, safe and sound."

"You buried the prince in the dirt?" Ryan stated as a look of shock washed across his face.

"Well, he couldn't go into battle with us, could he?" She replied rather smugly as she used her shirt to wipe down the, nowmore dirt than golden, egg. "Besides, a little dirt never hurt." She smiled at Ryan haughtily.

Ryan, stunned at her boldness, began to reply when they heard the ghastly sound of thunder once more, this time it was flowed by a flash of fire!

Ryan knew that could only mean one thing... Darkness! She was alive and she was back with a vengeance!

Ryan snatched Ellie by the hand and practically dragged her to the back of the tunnel. They crouched down as Ryan quickly began to rub dirt across his shield.

"What are you doing?" Ellie whispered, realizing too that they were still not free from Darkness.

"We can hide behind my shield, but I don't want it giving us away," he said as he covered the last bit of shine and pulled it firmly against them. "We will hide and hope that she either leaves or help arrives."

"Gee," said Ellie with a bit of sarcasm. "That is a good plan."

Ryan smirked at her sarcasm as he tucked the crystal into his pocket, causing them to once again be cloaked in black.

Flashes of light flickered as Darkness snorted fire into various passages one at a time.

"She seems to be getting closer," said Ellie in a whisper.

Ryan put Ellie's arm around his own as they braced themselves to face Darkness. "We will be okay," he said confidently. "Remember the good guys always win." *Please let that really be true!*

Ryan carefully peeked out from behind the shield. He could see a little bit, from the small fires now burning in the cave. Another flash of light shot across the entrance to the small passage.

"I think she is blowing fire into the tunnels, trying to find us," Ryan whispered to Ellie.

Ellie closed her eyes tightly and gripped Ryan's arm.

Sniff, snort, and sniff.

"What was that?" Ellie whispered.

"It sounds like the smoke may be getting to Darkness too," replied Ryan trying to held back a cough.

"Come out, come out where ever you are," roared the evil voice of Darkness.

Sniff, snort and sniff.

They held their breath as they heard her stick her head into the tunnel where they were hiding.

Sniff, snort, and sniff.

"Ahh, little ones," Darkness said softly. "Do I smell a certain flower that grows only in the royal gardens?"

Ellie tensed up as she pulled the small flower bud from her pocket and gripped it tightly in her hand, trying to contain the fragrant odor.

"Seems to be an odd place for shuv-zachar to grow," mocked Darkness. "Come out and give me the prince, and I shall let the girl live… as my pet."

Ryan and Ellie remained quiet and still. Neither knew just what they should do.

Darkness, annoyed with their failure to submit, discharged a large stream of fire into the narrow tunnel. Ryan braced the shield with his feet at the intense force of the fire. Ellie squeezed his arm even tighter as she tried not to scream.

Just as Ryan felt the strength deplete from his legs against the torrent of fire, it suddenly ceased. Ryan fell limp as his strength left him.

Ellie grabbed the shield from his frail hand. "Ryan, are you okay?" she whispered.

Before Ryan could answer a loud noise roared, like waves crashing upon a tin wall. Flashes of light filled the tunnel, and the ground trembled.

Ellie dropped the shield and looked out. She could barely make out what appeared to be two dragons caught up in intense battle. With a flash of light, she realized that it was Ashmond! He had come to save them!

She looked over at Ryan's limp body and struck him hard across the face. "OUCH!" he cried out in shock!

"Hurry," she replied in haste. "Pull yourself together. We must get the prince to safety!"

Ryan, still weak, and now very annoyed, cradled the precious egg and followed Ellie.

Ashmond saw the two brave young souls as they fled from the small passage. He turned to Darkness and gave a mighty blow to shut her eyes and give them cover in which to escape. Ryan and Ellie saw their chance and made their way out of there as quick as they could!

Armed soldiers met them at the ornate door. "Quick," yelled out one of the soldiers to another. "Get them to safety! Everyone else, save the king!"

Home Again

Evening settled in as Ryan found himself back in the grand throne room of the castle.

He stood, waiting patiently, in the middle of the room next to the Queen, for Ellie to finish changing. He pulled at the hideous frilly collar that hugged his neck like a hangman's noose. *I can't believe that this is all the queen had for me to wear.* Ryan's hand fell to his side as Ellie entered the room. She looked like an angel. There were no words to describe her beauty at that moment. Her golden blonde hair framed her porcelain face with wide curls infused with flowers. Her blue eyes sparkled like the lavish gems that adorned her full teal and purple dress. The rich gold trim seemed to light up the room around her. She glowed like an angel as she walked towards him.

"Are you wearing tights?" she giggled as she wrapped her arm with his.

Ryan could not respond. He was speechless.

Ellie continued to giggle at the silly look on Ryan's face.

Stomp, Stomp!

The harsh blow of Capula's golden staff hitting the solid marble floor returned Ryan to his senses.

"Announcing King Ashmond," boomed Capula, staff in hand.

The king entered the throne room, leaning heavily on an elaborately carved cane. His massive body seemed almost too much for such a small piece of wood. He had suffered only minor injuries during his encounter with Darkness, but they took their toll on him yet. It was an intense battle. The king and soldiers fought valiantly, but Darkness managed to escape the fate of death once again. She stole from Ellie's playbook and escaped down a secret passageway after causing an avalanche of her own.

Ashmond made his way to the throne and signaled for Ellie and Ryan to come near. "We have survived another attack from Darkness, and I am glad to see that you are safe." Ashmond motioned for the royal soldiers to leave the room. "I still do not know how she knew that you were here. It is clear that we have a spy within our castle walls."

Ryan and Ellie could not imagine why anyone would want to go against the King and side with Darkness.

Ashmond continued after letting go of a long sigh, as though he were trying to release the weight of the World from his shoulders. "I have so many things that I need to tell you about the quest before you, but time is running out, so please listen closely."

Ashmond went on to explain that each dragon is granted a gift of up to five crystals from the heavens to give them their powers. Most common dragons are blessed with one or maybe two crystals, such as the gift of flight, or of fire. Only those of the royal bloodline are bestowed more. It has been several generations since more than three gifts have been bestowed to a dragon. The power is too great. Prophecy has foretold though that our little prince shall receive an abundance of gifts, this is why Darkness longs to control him. He shall grow to be the most powerful dragon in nearly 2000 years.

The first crystal appeared just after the birth of a royal dragon egg. Ryan remembered the story Grandpa had told him under the stars, it all made sense. It is the crystal of unity. It binds the dragon to his protector and allows travel between our worlds. This crystal is only granted to the first-born egg of every royal family. It is our most precious gift, as it unites our worlds. It can also alert the protector if his dragon brother is in danger or needs him, and vice versa.

The rest of the crystals contain the gifts of the four elements that God spoke during creation; wind, fire, earth and water.

"You must return the young prince to Dragon World to receive his next crystal. The unity crystal will glow when the time draws near, but if at any point you need return, just take hold of the crystal and the young prince, the crystal will know of your wish to return," said Ashmond.

"Now, it is time. You must go quickly, before Darkness returns," concluded Ashmond as he rose from his throne and ushered Ryan and Ellie back toward the mighty drawbridge.

"Wait," cried Ryan. "I cannot go, not without Grandpa. I know Darkness still has him. She said that she would kill him, which means he is still alive! We must go and save him."

"I know this is hard for you," replied Ashmond, "but you must get the prince to safety. I promise, we will do all that is within us to save Grandpa. He is my closest friend. We are as brothers, and I will save him even if it costs me my life."

Ellie took Ryan by the hand, "Ashmond will do as he promises. Please, let's go home."

Ryan knew that she wanted to go home. He did too! He missed his parents, and Grandma, and yes, he even missed his sister. He solemnly nodded his head as they crossed over the mighty drawbridge.

Ryan looked up at the red sky. The stars seemed to speak to him, calling him home. With a heavy heart, he held the crystal up toward the heavens and it began to glow bright. He looked over at the Queen as she began to weep.

"I promise, I will guard him with my life," he pledged, trying to comfort her, as he nestled the egg gently into the safety of his shirt. He knew that it was as hard for the queen to see the prince go, as it was for him to leave his grandpa.

Ellie and Ryan joined hands, as the light of the crystal grew. The stars began to spin faster and faster. Then, they were back at Grandma's house just as suddenly as they had left.

They looked around the room. The sun was just beginning to rise. They heard the sound of the rooster crow. Ryan pulled the egg from his shirt and cradled it in his arms just as the bedroom door opened. It was Grandma.

"You have returned," she said in amazement. "And you have the prince?" she gazed in awe at the precious golden egg. "I saw a glow coming from under your door last night. I rushed to your room, but you were already gone." Grandma said as she bowed her head as though she had failed an important task.

Ryan rushed to hold her and comfort her. *I am the one that has failed.*

"I saw that you had the magnifying glass in the hall earlier," Grandma continued. "But where on Earth did you find your Dragon crystal? It belonged to the prince. Ashmond had given it to Grandpa after we had made plans to take you to Dragon World. I used it to go back there to make plans to take you to Dragon World myself and retrieve the royal dragon egg. I have not been able to find it anywhere! I was so worried!"

Ryan opened his hand and showed it to her. "It was in the old tree by the barn," he replied.

"I must have dropped it after my last visit to Dragon World. I had gone to the barn to get your great grandpa Milton's chest out to show you and explain to you that Dragon World needs your help." Grandma said as she then began to look around the room, in search of her husband.

Ryan and Ellie looked at each other. Ellie walked over to Grandma and Ryan and pulled the flower from her hair.

"He is still a prisoner of Darkness," she replied softly. "But Ashmond has sworn to save him."

Ellie then placed the shuv-zachar flower into Grandmas hand. Grandma held it to her nose and smiled.

"Thank you," she said to Ellie. "I'm sure you two are very tired. I will answer all your questions after you have rested." Grandma closed the door behind her as she left. Ryan knew she was disappointed, but was glad to see the smile upon her face.

"Well," Ellie said as she ran her hands over her beautiful new dress. "I suppose I better change and lay down for a bit. I know you must be tired."

"Are you kidding?" replied Ryan. "How could you possibly sleep after what we have just been through?"

Ellie smiled, she had not really wanted to go to bed.

They quickly plopped down on the bed and placed the egg upon it.

"Have you decided on a name?" Ellie asked with excitement.

Ryan smiled, held up the egg, and whispered the name,

"SHADOW."